TO:

Jaclyn

WHO I ADMIRE.

FROM:

Anna

WHO YOU INSPIRE.

For Nicole Kaplan—The world has gained an incredible teacher.
—P.R.

Dedicated to Ms. Simons, Mrs. Ratte, and Mrs. White.
Thank you for your brilliant light
and for showing Linden a rainbow of possibilities.
We will forever love and remember you.

—H.H.

ISBN 978-0-06-301274-5

The artist used digital media to create the illustrations for this book.
Typography by Jeanne L. Hogle
21 22 23 24 25 PC 10 9 8 7 6 5 4 3 2 1

First Edition

Dear Teacher,

A Celebration of People Who Inspire Us

by PARIS ROSENTHAL   illustrated by HOLLY HATAM

HARPER

An Imprint of HarperCollinsPublishers

Dear Teacher,

THAN

K YOU.

Just because.

The Power of YET!

I can't do this...YET

I'm not good at this...YET

KINDNESS MATTERS

Dear Teacher,

I'm grateful for all that you do.

Dear Teacher,

Thank you for noticing that I love to dream big
and encouraging me to do exactly that.

Dear Teacher,

You make me feel like I matter, no matter what.

Dear Teacher,

You're super kind,

you're super cool,

and you're my superhero!

Dear Teacher,

Sometimes we show,

sometimes we tell—

LET'S BE FRIENDS!

you taught me the importance of both.

Dear Teacher,

Because of you, I know when to take a

DEEP BREATH in . . .

and when to let it out.

Dear Teacher,

You inspire me to inspire others.

Dear Teacher,

You taught me to

PASS THE BALL,

even when I think I have the shot.

Dear Teacher,

You have seen me fly,

you have seen me fall.

Thank you for being there wherever I land.

Dear Teacher,

Thank you for showing me that it's smart to think outside the box.

Dear Teacher,

You taught me that there are many paths to take.

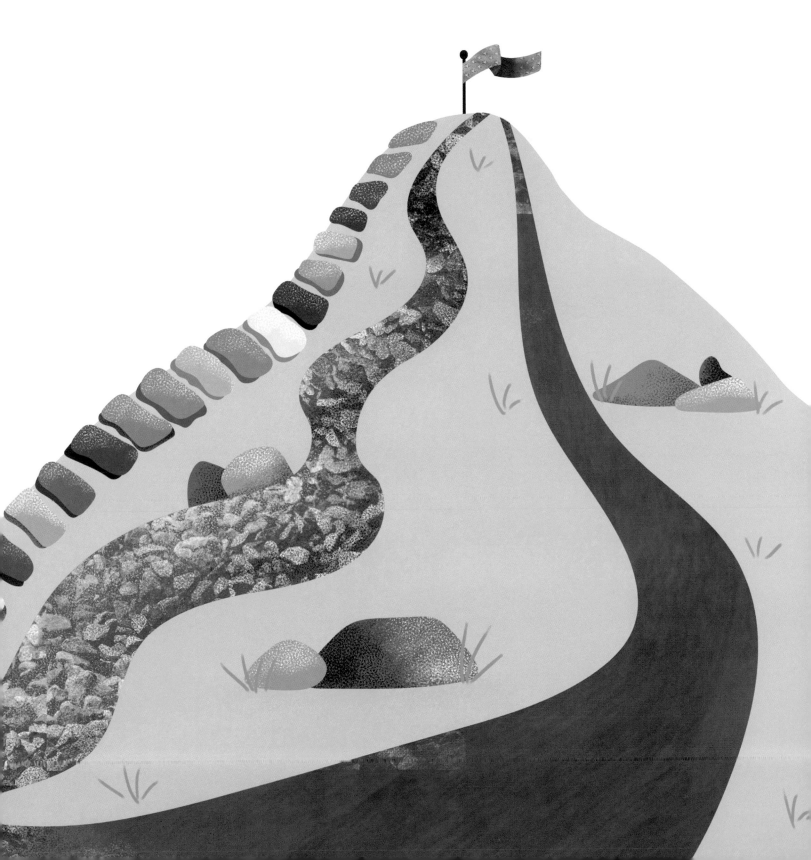

Dear Teacher,

Thank you for lifting me up,
thank you for never letting me down,

and thank you for sending me on my way!

Dear Teacher,

You are a gift that keeps on giving,
and this book is my gift to you.

Most of all, dear teacher who I admire,
thank you for making me feel like I can

always

always

always . . .

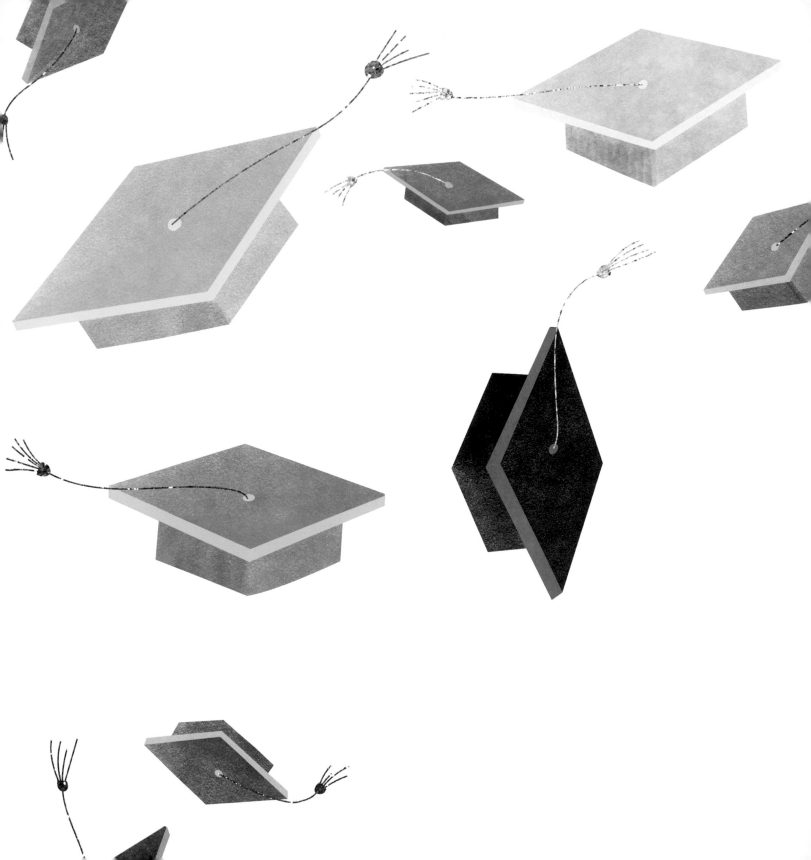

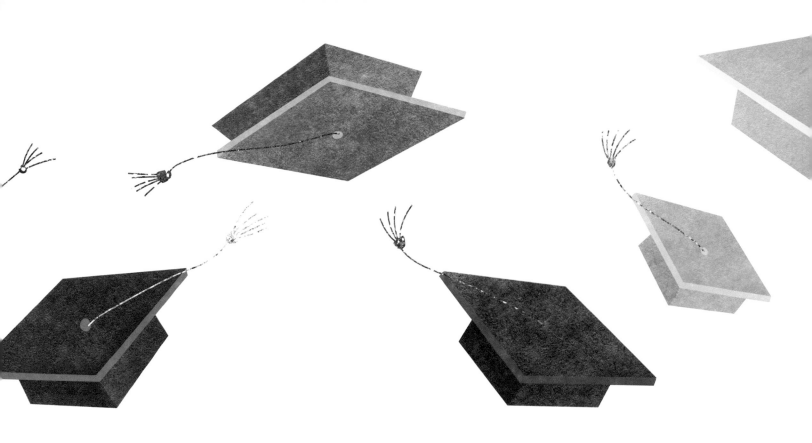

count on you.